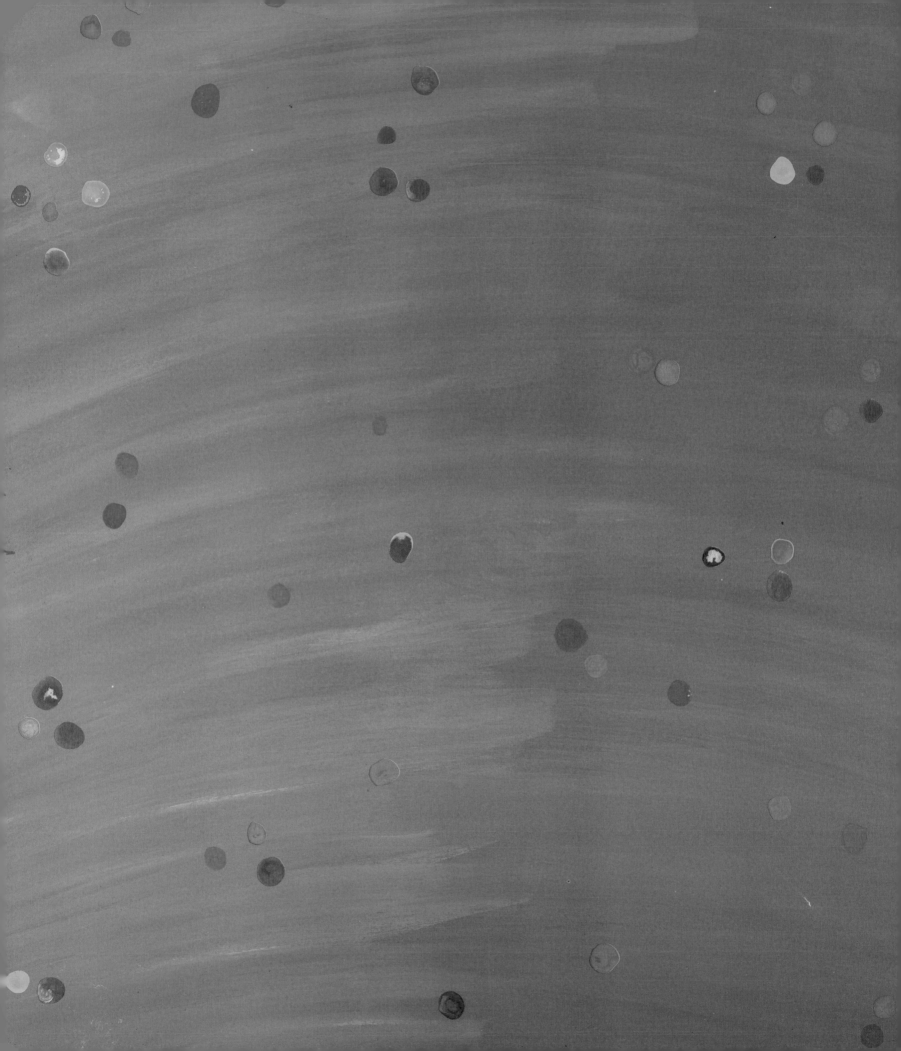

Vera B. Williams

"MORE MORE MORE," SAID THE BABY

3 LOVE STORIES

A Mulberry Paperback Book  New York

This book consists of gouache paintings. The
lettering was done as part of the paintings by the
artist with the valuable assistance
of Savannah T. Etheredge.
It is based on Gill Sans Extra Bold.

The Library of Congress has cataloged the
Greenwillow Books edition of
"More More More," Said the Baby as follows:

Williams, Vera B.
"More more more," said the baby / Vera B. Williams.
p. cm.
Summary: Three babies are caught up in the air
and given loving attention by a father,
grandmother, and mother.
ISBN 0-688-09173-3. ISBN 0-688-09174-1 (lib. bdg.)
[1. Babies—Fiction. 2. Parent and child—Fiction.]
I. Title. PZ7.W6685Mo 1990 [E]—dc19 89-2023 CIP AC

3 5 7 9 10 8 6 4
First Mulberry Edition, 1996
ISBN 0-688-14736-4

For Hudson

For William

For Rebecca

For August

For Clare

and for all grandchildren

This is Little Guy.

Little Guy runs away so fast

Little Guy's daddy
has to run like anything
just to catch that baby up.

But Little Guy's daddy catches that baby up all right.

He throws that baby high

"Just look at you
with your perfect belly button

right in the middle
right in the middle
right in the middle
of your fat little belly."

and gives that little guy's belly

a kiss right in the middle
of the belly button.

"More," laughs Little Guy.

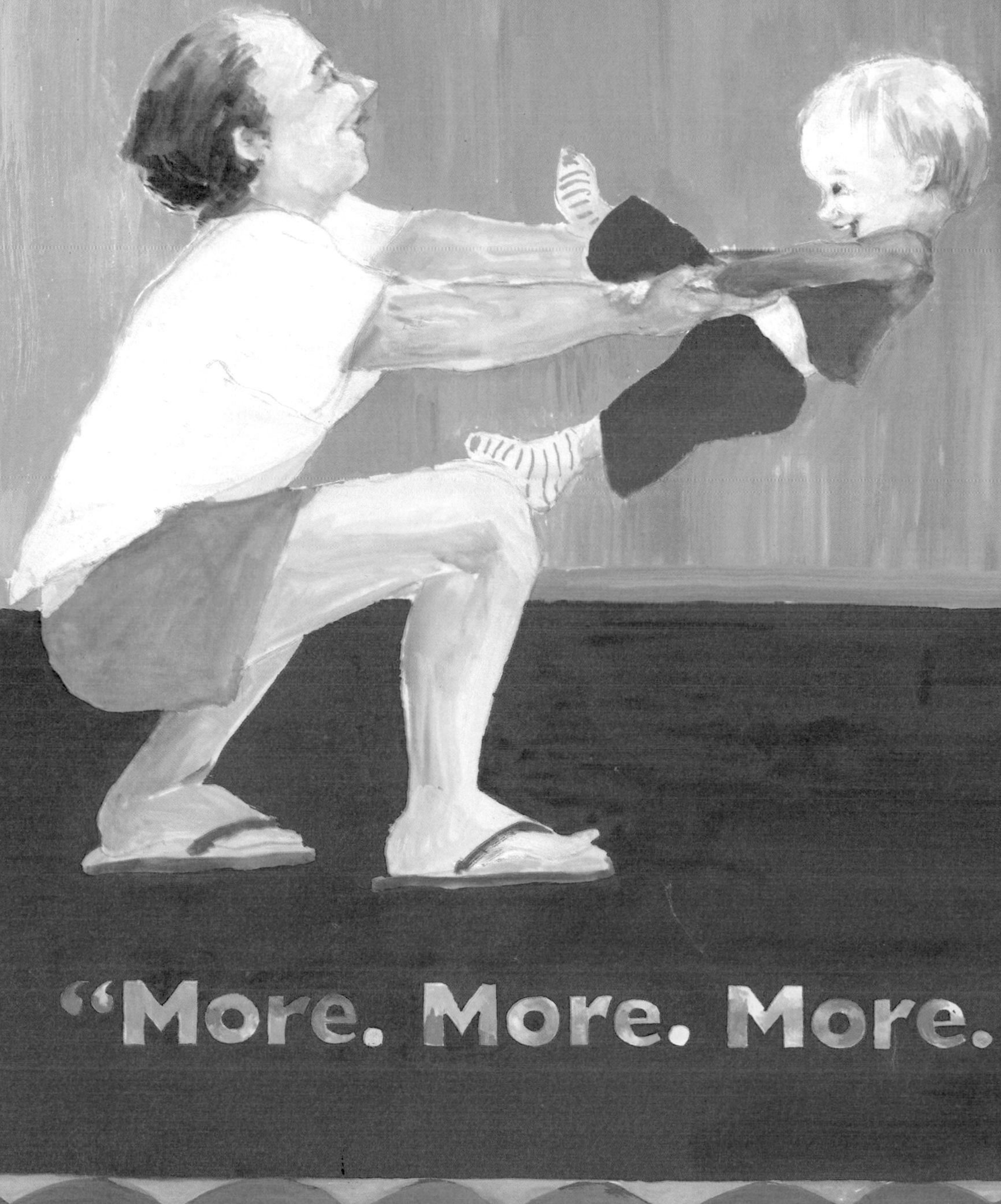

"More. More. More."

LITTLE PUMPKIN

Now this is Little Pumpkin.

Little Pumpkin scoots away so fast

Little Pumpkin's grandma
has to run like anything
just to catch that baby up.

But Little Pumpkin's grandma
catches that baby up all right.

She holds that baby nose to nose

and swings that baby all around.

"Oh my best little grandbaby,"
Little Pumpkin's grandma
sings to Little Pumpkin.

"Just look at you
with your ten little toes

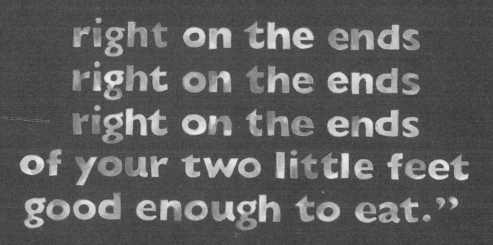

right on the ends
right on the ends
right on the ends
of your two little feet
good enough to eat."

Then Little Pumpkin's grandma
brings that baby right up close

and tastes each
of Little Pumpkin's toes.

"More," laughs Little Pumpkin.
"More. More. More."

LITTLE BIRD

Now comes Little Bird.

Little Bird falls asleep so fast

Little Bird's mama
has to move like anything
just to catch that baby up.

But Little Bird's mama
lifts that baby in her arms all right.
She rocks that baby back and forth

and gets that baby ready for bed.

"Oh my best little baby,"
Little Bird's mama
sings to Little Bird.

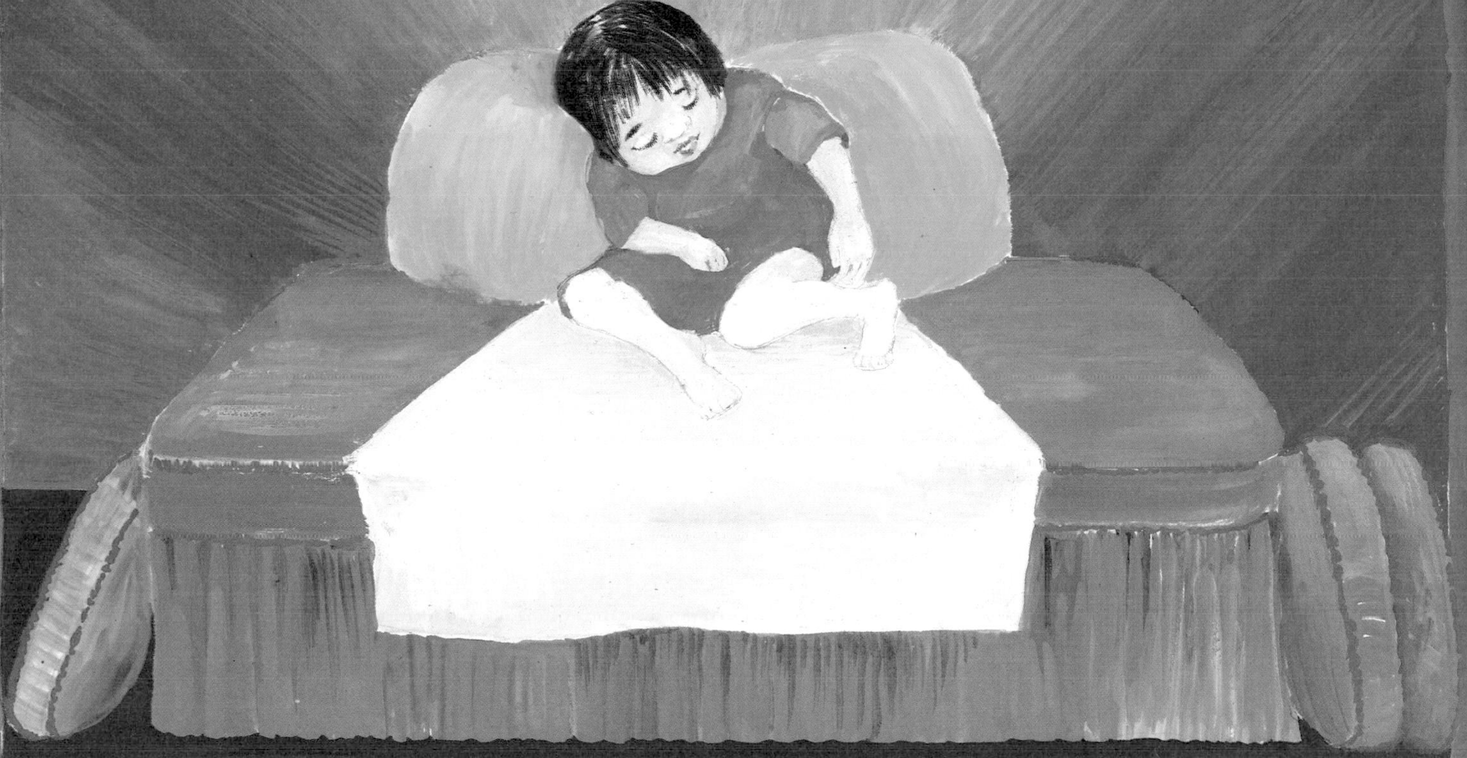

Then Little Bird's mama
brings that baby right up close.

She gives that little bird a kiss
right on each of her little eyes.

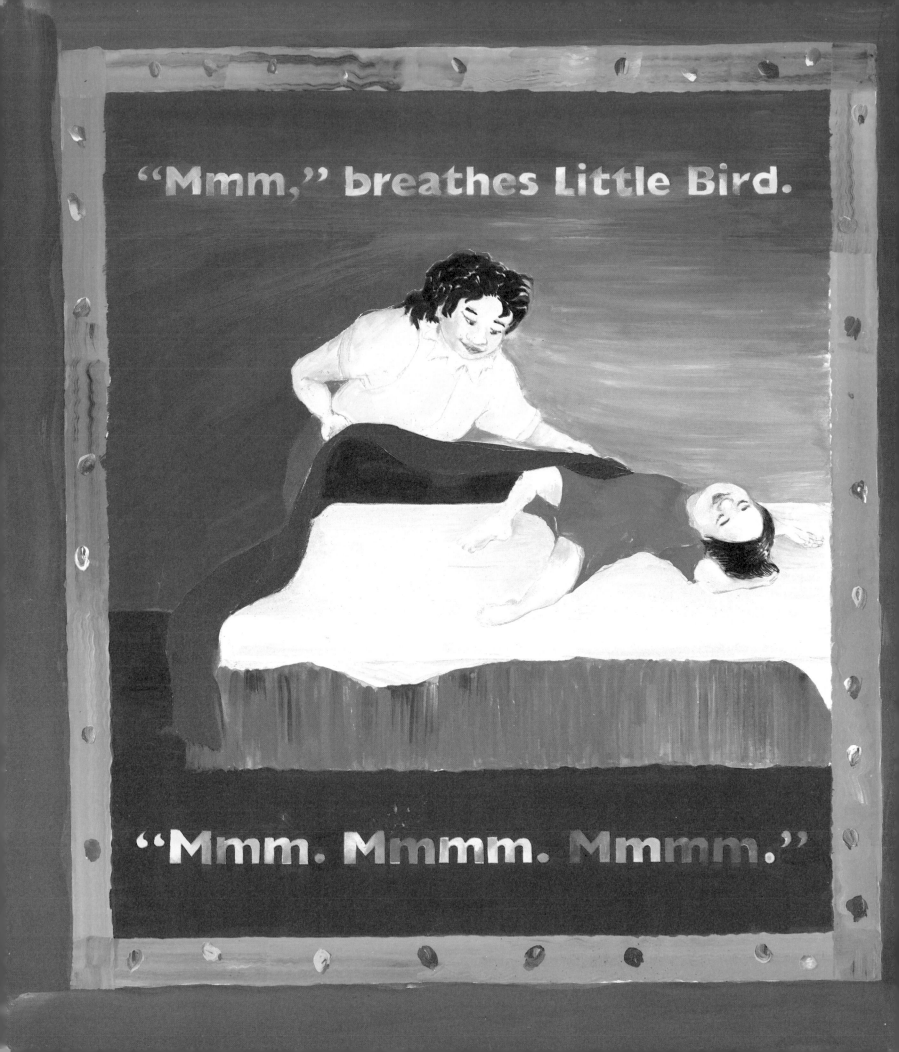

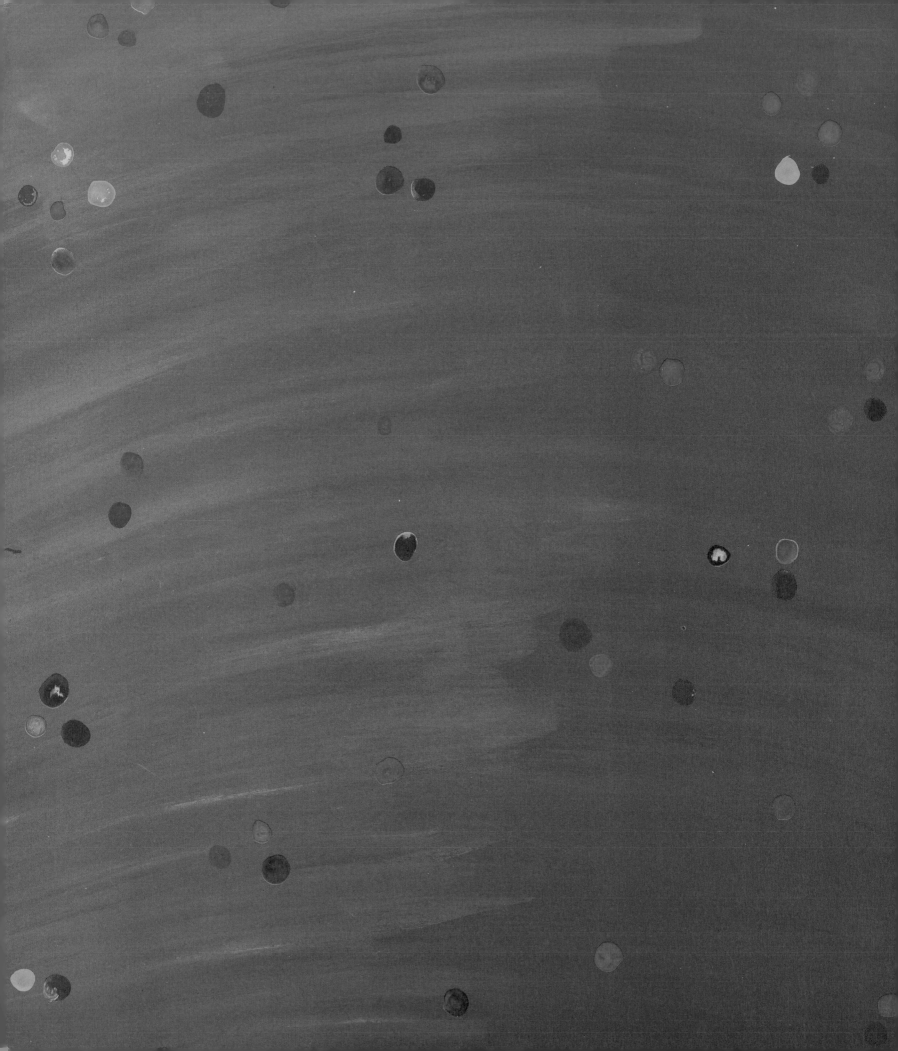